Twits Abroad

A Steampunk Distraction

Tom Alan Robbins

Book Three of THE TWITS CHRONICLES

What People Are Saying:

"The Twits Chronicles are hilarious, blessed with truly exceptional dialogue. Steampunk dystopia meets Oscar Wildean wit in these books. I found myself laughing out loud on numerous occasions--and that's not something I often do while reading. " **—Nick Sullivan**, author of The Deep Series and Zombie Bigfoot.

"Delightful! A frothy frappe of P.G. Wodehouse and steam-punk. If you're the sort who reads blurbs before reading the book, stop it. Stop it right now. Read TWITS IN LOVE and have a good time. These days we can all use a bit more of a good time." **—John Ostrander**, American writer of comic books, including *Suicide Squad, Grimjack* and *Star Wars: Legacy.*

"I haven't enjoyed the company of such eccentric characters since A Confederacy of Dunces, and Tom Alan Robbins has managed to place them in the stylized world of Oscar Wilde. A really unique journey." — **Kevin Conroy**, Actor, The voice behind the DC Comics superhero Batman .

"Tom Alan Robbins' Twits stories are hilarious, thought provoking and mind bending. His juicy turns of phrase will stick in your ear like a catchy song." — **Michael Urie**, Actor, Producer and Director

"Tom is the most talented, delicious writer. Do yourself a favor, and immerse yourself in the fabulous world of TWITS!" — **Mary Testa**, 3 time Tony Award Nominee

The Author makes no representation of any kind as to his being a citizen of the United Kingdom, either native or naturalized. He is from a small town in Ohio, for which he apologizes.

Copyright © 2022 by Tom Alan Robbins

This is a work of fiction. All events described are imaginary; all characters are entirely fictitious and are not intended to represent actual living persons.

Cover design by Melody J. Barber of Aurora Publicity

Additional designs by Eric Wright of The Puppet Kitchen.

Twits Logo designed by Feppa Rodriquez

Proofreading by Gretchen Tannert Douglas

For Noreen O'Neil, who spotted this story headed for the precipice and gently placed it back on the tracks. Her warmth, generosity and insight added immeasurably to the success of these books.

Contents

ONE

The Horrors of Euphonia Gumboot

I don't know if you've heard of this Isaac Newton chap, but apparently, he had brains positively leaking out of his ears. He said something to the effect that for everything pleasant that happens, there will be something equally beastly lurking around the corner. This is the only scientific fact I have retained from my school days, and time has proven it true. There I was, happily downing Cook's warm scones with cherry preserves and washing them down with the old lapsang souchong when Bentley slid in with the news that my Aunt Hypatia was chewing the furniture in the parlor and demanding to see me. Bentley, if you are meeting him for the first time, is a steam-powered domestic with a stately dome and an air of moral certainty that will brook no opposition.

"What does my aunt want? Did she say?"

"She did not, although I was able to discern the phrases, 'young pup' and 'cease this shilly-shallying' from amidst the general verbiage."

"This bodes ill. You couldn't tell her I have appendicitis?"

"I could not."

Experience has taught me that making my aunt wait only allows the venom to accumulate in her fangs. I sighed and took a final bite of scone. "May as well take the ball by the horns, what?"

Bentley raised an eyebrow. "Bull, Sir."

"Pardon?"

"One takes the bull by the horns. Balls do not typically have horns."

I thought this over for a tick. "What's a bull?"

"A bull was a male cow, Sir."

"Damn the Great Extinction!"

Bentley assumed a professorial tone. "It was also used to refer to the male of several other extinct species, including elephants."

That perked me up. I love being able to spread out what few nuggets of scholarly wisdom I possess for all to admire. "I am acquainted with elephants. They were known for holding grudges."

He tilted his head. "For remembering, Sir. I don't believe there was any malice involved."

"Then my aunt is certainly not an elephant. Her memory is used exclusively for mischief."

Bentley gave a little sigh. "We're rather losing the thread."

"It was you that brought up elephants."

"I apologize most abjectly. It was entirely my fault."

"You're being too hard on yourself as usual, Bentley. Well, let's see what the old girl wants."

My Aunt Hypatia could be called a dragon in that her scaly exterior is impervious to attack and that she breathes fire when aroused. Bentley's intelligence had led me to expect a certain Visigoth flavour in my aunt's demeanor so I was surprised to find her smiling at me as if I were a shining example of natural selection.

"Good morning, Aunt. Confusion to our enemies."

"Cyril, darling! Is that the new motto?"

"According to Bentley."

"I think he can be trusted. Confusion to our enemies. Let me look at you."

I was happy to oblige as it required no effort from me. After regarding me up and down, the bottom of her face formed a smile while the upper half held a private meeting to discuss its findings.

"You look tired. Are you getting enough sleep?"

"Oodles. I'm really making an effort!"

"You've lost weight. Do you still employ that eccentric cook of yours?"

"I've gained three pounds and it was worth every mouthful thanks to what you call my 'eccentric cook.'"

"And that mechanical servant of yours—don't you find that these older models require endless amounts of maintenance?"

The alarm bells began clanging in my noggin. She clearly had an agenda, and that was bound to be hard luck for me.

"Bentley does his own maintenance."

She pursed her lips judiciously. "I have thought for some time that Bentley is not a good influence on you."

A cold sweat began to gather on the nape of my neck. "Bentley is indispensable. I would sooner part with my thumbs than Bentley."

My aunt waved away my objections. "Well, thumbs are over-rated anyway. A gentleman should use his thumbs as little as possible. That is what servants are for."

"He practically raised me, after all."

"That is no recommendation. His code made it impossible for him to discipline you and because he himself is a mechanism he was incapable of teaching you how humans actually behave. Consequently you are like a dog that is raised to believe it is a person and views other dogs with amused condescension. No, I'm afraid that cannot be counted among Bentley's accomplishments."

I desperately tried to shunt her off onto a side track.

"How's Uncle Hugo? I trust you left him well?"

"I left him adding and subtracting in his little office. He can do no harm in there and will emerge exhausted, which is ideal. A well-rested husband is the Devil's plaything. You should take up some enervating hobbies yourself."

It was high time to take the ball by the horns. Sorry... bull. "Look here, Aunt, why this sudden interest in my domestic affairs?"

"It seems to me that this higgledy-piggledy bachelor life you lead is taking a terrible toll on you. I am naturally concerned."

"And I suppose your remedy is to attach some weak-eyed barnacle like Euphonia Gumboot to me in matrimony?"

My aunt glared down her nose at me. "Euphonia Gumboot is the daughter of my oldest friend. I consider that recommendation enough. If you feel any sense of obligation for the affection I have lavished upon you since childhood, you will oblige me by marrying her at once."

"I don't like her."

She smiled with satisfaction. "You see? It's as if you've been married for years. She will take you in hand."

"I don't want to be taken in hand. I'm quite happy as I am."

"You are not. No man who possesses youth, money and freedom can be happy until those things are taken away by a loving partner. We never appreciate a thing until it is gone. It is like the pang one feels upon eating the last chocolate in the box—even inferior chocolate leaves one with a certain wistfulness."

"Euphonia Gumboot is a blight and a pestilence."

"She is waiting in the car."

"You don't think I'm going to invite her in?"

"Of course not. I have already done so."

"Really, Aunt!"

"You left me no choice. You possess the skills of a Houdini."

Bentley drifted in and cleared his throat. "Miss Euphonia Gumboot, Sir."

Have you ever gazed into a lively brook and noticed how the water merrily twists and fractures the images of the submerged rocks? Euphonia was rather like that.

She had all the required features but one found oneself reaching for corrective lenses before realizing that the problem was not one's eyes. I took a deep breath.

"Euphonia! I hope I see you well."

"Can you not see me well? I can move into the light." She staggered a few paces toward the window. "Is that better?"

It was definitely not. "Um, yes."

My aunt attempted to impose order. "Come and sit down, my dear. You and my nephew are acquainted, I believe?"

"Are we? Who is your nephew?"

Aunt Hypatia's composure slipped the tiniest bit. "This is my nephew... Cyril."

"Oh! I thought you were speaking of another nephew."

"Why would I... never mind. Why don't you gaze at that clock on the wall? It shows your profile to its best advantage."

"All right. Confusion is our enemy."

"I suppose you mean confusion to our enemies."

"Is that it?"

"It is."

I thought I'd better swing the conversation to something more cheerful. "Confusion to our enemies. So, Aunt, are you going to the country this weekend?"

"We are not. I am holding a little soiree here in town tomorrow night which you will be so good as to attend."

"Tomorrow night? Drat! How I'd love to be there but..."

"Cease these fruitless machinations. You must be part eel, upon my word. It is not enough to get you into the boat. One must strike you with an oar to be sure of you."

I slumped in defeat. "Who will be at this soiree, might one ask?"

"Oh, people... it's rather a potpourri."

Euphonia spoke without removing her eyes from the clock. "I'll be there."

Aunt Hypatia glared at the back of her head. "I'm afraid you've sprung the trap before the mouse had time to smell the cheese, my dear."

"What?"

My aunt sighed. "Yes, that's roughly the level of comprehension I anticipated."

"Really, Aunt."

"You may bring your cousin Cheswick if that will make the evening more palatable."

Cheswick Wickford-Davies (Binky to his familiars) is as much a responsibility as a friend. He has an unfortunate tendency to put his foot in it, and over the years I have pulled said foot out of many a sticky situation. He is loyal and unfailingly chipper, however, and blood is thicker than water, although I have yet to see the scientific evidence. Euphonia made a sound like a discontented kitten.

"I'm getting a crick in my neck."

"Just another moment, my dear. Observe the intricate gilding on the second hand."

"Which is the second hand?"

"The larger one, I believe."

"So the other is the first hand?"

My aunt stared at the back of her head. "Why not?"

"Can I offer you tea?" I asked insincerely. "Cook has made some scones."

"No thank you. As you know, I distrust anything that has not been inspected in a government facility."

"You don't know what you're missing."

"What I do not know cannot hurt me. Ignorance is like a shining shield in that regard. Well, we should take our leave. Until tomorrow night."

"Are we going? Can I stop looking at the clock now?"

"Yes, dear. I think it's best you not speak again until we're in the car. Let us preserve what tattered mystery we still possess."

"What?"

"Precisely. Ta-ta, Nephew."

"Yes. Ta-ta. Love and all that."

I saw them to the door with the usual flourishes and watched them drive off with a sinking feeling in my vitals. "Bentley?"

"Sir?"

"You heard?"

"Yes, Sir."

"What shall I do?"

"I have been meditating on the subject and my suggestion is that you should go abroad."

I looked at him doubtfully. "Really? Can I do that?"

"Among your recent correspondence there was an invitation to attend a conference on matters of a vaguely scientific nature."

"Zounds, that sounds deadly."

"I believe it is the custom to frame these invitations as dry academic events, but the reality involves a great deal more alcohol than is implied in the letter."

"That's more like it. Where is this convocation?"

"New York, Sir."

"Hallo! Now you're talking."

"The opening ceremony is tomorrow evening. If you are not to be tardy you must leave today."

"Perfect! I'll miss my aunt's soiree completely."

"That is my understanding."

"But even the fastest ship will never make it in time."

"You could take your dirigible, Sir."

I stared at him in wonder. "I have a dirigible?"

"Smythe Corporation possesses several dirigibles for purposes of publicity and executive junkets. As the owner of the company, they are at your disposal."

"Pack my things and tell the airfield to gas up the spiffiest blimp on the lot."

"At once, Sir."

The doorbell chose that moment to play "Lady of Spain." A fast-talking salesman had convinced me that musical doorbells were the coming thing. Apparently, they were still en route.

"You don't suppose my aunt has returned?"

"I shall ascertain who it is."

He misted away and condensed back into the room with my cousin Binky slouching behind him looking as if fortune and he had parted on bad terms.

"Hallo, old cock! What brings you to the ancestral home on this fine morn? Confusion to our enemies."

"Not 'Death before dishonour'?"

"It's the latest thing, I'm told."

"Confusion to our enemies, then. I'm up a tree, Cyril."

"Put your foot in it, have you?"

"What I did I was compelled to do by the dictates of natural law."

"Which natural law are we speaking of?"

"The law of animal attraction. We have glands, haven't we? And those glands require us to obey certain urges, don't they? And if a young person takes things the wrong way it can cause a certain amount of trouble, can't it?"

"Why don't you start at the beginning with as few rhetorical flourishes as possible?"

"Lady of Spain" echoed through the halls once again. Bentley passed us at a gliding run. "Excuse me, Sir."

I turned back to Binky, whose eyes were growing feverish. "Continue, old duck."

"Well, you know I'm terribly keen on Judy."

"A fine young lady."

"I happened to be standing next to her on a balcony in the moonlight..."

"Dangerous things—balconies. Started all that trouble with Romeo and Juliet."

"And moonlight is the very devil for rousing romantic feelings in a chap."

"I avoid it like poison oak."

Bentley passed us again, moving at a more stately pace.

"Who was it, Bentley?"

"No one, Sir."

"No one?"

"No, Sir."

"Odd. That's been happening quite a lot lately. Perhaps the bell is broken."

"Perhaps, Sir."

"I'm getting rather tired of 'Lady of Spain,' I must say."

"I could acquire a new bell with a more conventional ring."

"Stay the course, Bentley. Musical doorbells will come into their own shortly and we shall be the envy of all and sundry."

"No doubt, Sir."

He glided to the side table and began polishing knickknacks, looking rather gloomy, I thought. I turned back to Binky. "Sorry, go on, old man. You were standing in the perilous moonlight..."

"We were chatting away and I suddenly found myself getting lost in her eyes. Before I knew it, I had said something that in retrospect sounded very like a proposal."

"What was the exact wording? Imagine I'm your divorce lawyer. What did you say?"

"That's the thing... I can't remember. Between the moonlight and those eyes, it's all rather vague. It was something along the lines of, 'A chap would be pretty bally lucky to spend his life with someone like you...' and then there might have been, 'I wish I could stand here in the moonlight with you forever.' I might have thrown in something like, 'Do you think you could ever go for a sap like me?'"

"And what was her reply?"

"Again, it's all rather foggy. I think she said, 'Sure.'"

"Simple and to the point."

"But did she believe she was accepting a proposal? It's a rather important thing to ferret out."

"You could do worse."

"I barely know her. We've never even gone to dinner. And I have nothing to offer her. As you know, the old coffers are bare."

"I don't think she cares about money."

He looked at me with alarm. "You see? What other horrible secrets is she hiding?"

"Let's find out if she considers herself engaged. If the answer is no then these concerns are moot. Say, here's an idea..."

Binky cleared his throat theatrically. He widened his eyes and jerked his head significantly toward Bentley.

I stared at him blankly. "What on earth are you doing?"

"It's just... are you sure you wouldn't like to ask Bentley?"

Bentley's joints gave a little squeak. "I would be happy to help, Sir."

"Stand down, Bentley. I have a perfect plan."

He stepped back rather slower than he had stepped forth. "Of course, Sir."

Binky stared at me desperately. "But... really? I mean, he's right there... devious as a Medici. 'Happy to help,' he said."

"Not necessary. Trust in me, old badger."

"I feel a little nauseous. Perhaps I should sit down."

He flopped into a chair and slumped despairingly. I hastened to reassure him.

"I'm leaving today for New York in the company dirigible to attend a scientific conference."

He looked at me oddly. "That's a lot to digest in one sentence."

"I'm taking Cook, of course. It would make perfect sense to ask Judy to come as the officer in charge of social justice at Smythe Corporation. That makes it a kind of family junket."

I had found my genius of a cook, who by an odd coincidence was named Cook, on a recent adventure among the masses. Her children, Ernie and Judy, turned out to be rather brilliant as well and I had demonstrated my business acumen by hiring them.

"All those hours cooped up in the dirigible should sweat out Judy's true feelings."

My companion brightened at once. "And I'll get a free trip to New York!"

"Scurry home and pack. Meet us at the airfield at six."

"Righto! Thanks awfully, Cyril."

"Don't mention it, old rooster. Only too glad."

He trundled off happily. I pretended to stare at a stuffed owl on the mantel while focusing my peripheral vision on Bentley. Of course, I was dying to ask him what he thought of my plan, but pride—which bringeth down nations—made the old tongue cleave to the roof of one's mouth. His face was as smooth as a pot of mush.

"Well, Bentley, what are they wearing in New York these days?"

"The dress there is very different from what we are accustomed to. New Yorkers delight in disguising their wealth behind apparel that is as disreputable as possible. I believe dungarees and a T-shirt are all that are required, Sir."

"Even among tycoons?"

"Especially there, Sir. These captains of industry will certainly compete to see who can dress most authentically like a hobo."

"How odd. Well, whatever you think best. I rely on you."

"Thank you, Sir. Most gratifying. I shall begin packing at once."

He slid away like a pat of butter on a hot skillet. New York... with its legendary jazz clubs and belligerent pigeons. I was too excited to sit still. I paced the room, rearranging the knickknacks and then arranging them back again until I managed to drop a china figurine of a shepherdess and her swain, which shattered at once. Bentley leaned into the room and surveyed the damage.

"It will be several hours before we leave for the airfield, Sir."

"Yes, I'm well aware. Don't know what to do with myself. Bit excited, what?"

Bentley's gears ground for a moment. "I know it is a terrible imposition, Sir, but I wonder if I might ask you to untangle this ball of string? I am too occupied with packing to attend to it at the moment."

"String? Toss it this way. I'll have it untangled in no time. I'm an absolute wizard with string."

He rolled a large tangle of twine at me and I squinted at the various knots. The next thing I knew it was five o'clock and Bentley stood at the door with the suitcases. "Time to go? Oh well, I'll take care of that string when we return."

"Of course, Sir. The car is waiting."

I have a sad history of driving extravagant and fanciful vehicles but I had recently been shown the arrogance of flaunting my wealth in this obscene manner and now I drove about in a plain black sedan. Of course, the inside of the car was still fitted out like an Emperor's boudoir. Bentley drove as I rolled about on the satin bolsters nibbling Cook's peanut brittle. At last, we came to a halt.

"We have arrived, Sir."

I stepped from the back seat to behold a marvel. An enormous silver dirigible swung from its tethers before me. "Smythe Corporation" screamed from its side in bright red letters.

"Quite a sight, eh Bentley? Rather aggressively male, I must say. What makes it go up, do you suppose?"

"I believe the lift is supplied by hydrogen gas, Sir."

"What, the same stuff that lights up the sconces in the old domicile?"

"It is quite flammable, Sir."

I was seized by a sudden apprehension. "Flammable? Is there any danger?"

"It is perfectly safe, so long as there are no open flames aboard."

"What if it catches fire in the middle of the ocean? We'd be marooned."

"There is no possibility of being marooned."

"That's a relief."

"We would be incinerated instantly."

I goggled at him accusingly. "How gruesome! Attending my aunt's soiree only chanced indigestion and possible matrimony. This is a risk to life and limb."

Bentley stared into the middle distance.

"I believe I saw Cook carrying a large blueberry cobbler onto the airship, Sir."

I suddenly realized that I had not eaten a bite since breakfast. "Blueberry, you say?"

"With a streusel topping."

I straightened my shoulders. "Oh well, no one lives forever."

"Shall we board now, Sir?"

"Yes, let's have a look at this floating pleasure palace."

We climbed up the ramp and into the cabin. Overstuffed sofas and padded armchairs were scattered about among potted palms. It felt rather like my club, Twits. This impression was strengthened by the sight of C. Langford-Cheeseworth, a habitué of the club, lounging by a window and twirling his jeweled monocle.

"Cheeseworth? What are you doing here?"

Cheeseworth affected a rather louche manner of speaking. I had long suspected that his occasional inability to articulate the letter "R" was a theatrical device. "Hallo, Cywil. I'm a stowaway! What fun. I wan into Binky at the club and he told me all about your desperate flight to fweedom. I had to come along. Haven't been to New York in ages.

"So he was blabbing all over the club, was he?"

"Oh no. Just an intimate lunch. Consommé and cwackers. I'm sure no one overheard us."

"Well, welcome aboard, old duck."

"I lived in New York for a time in younger days. I had dweams of playing the saxophone in a low dive on the Bowery. Alas, my tongue lacked the necessary dexterity. I have labored on it since and now I can tie a cherry stem into a bow, but I still cannot play the saxophone."

He grew rather melancholy and stared out of the window. Cook was laying out a buffet. "Hallo, Cyril, love."

"Evening, Cook."

"Would you like some crostini with white beans, fresh thyme and olive oil?"

"Would I!"

I never missed a chance to swill down Cook's creations. Her crostini would make the angels weep. As

I started to load up a plate, I spotted Judy sitting in an armchair scribbling away in a notebook and Binky pretending not to stare at her from behind a palm plant. I sidled up to him, trying not to crunch too loudly on my crostini. "Well? Have you made any progress?"

He squinted at me myopically. "Not yet. I'm observing her behavior."

"How's that going?"

"My eyes are beginning to burn."

"Look here, you've got to get in there and roll about in the conversation if you're going to learn anything useful."

He looked up at me plaintively. "You do it."

"Me? I'm not the one in an ambiguous state of engagement."

"Just chat her up. See if she drops any hints."

"I'm not Mata Hari, you know."

His eyes grew moist. "I'd do it for you."

Well, I couldn't argue with that. Binky would do practically anything for anyone even if they expressly asked him not to.

"Very well, but don't expect miracles."

By now Judy had migrated to the buffet and was nibbling on a stuffed mushroom. I glided up next to her. "Quite a selection, what? The crostini are particularly savory."

"I've been snacking on Mum's crostini since I got my first tooth."

"Damned decent of you to come along on this junket."

"Thank you for asking me."

"Lots of opportunities to discuss social justice with like-minded individuals."

"Bentley gave me a list of the guests. It's packed with philanthropists. I've been making some notes."

"Good show. And what about you? Anything going on in your life that... you know, anything of a personal nature that's got you... I suppose one would say, is there anyone interesting in your personal life... of a personal nature?"

She gave me an odd look. "Are you trying to ask me if I'm seeing anyone?"

"Oh! Well... of course it's none of my business."

She looked down at the mushroom caps. "Isn't it?"

"If you'd rather not say..."

"You seem very interested."

"That's just my natural curiosity."

She glanced at me with a little smile. "You're so funny."

"Am I? I wish the fellows at the club thought so."

"You don't have to be so nervous."

"I'm not at all nervous. I'm cool as a cucumber."

I could see Binky watching us like a department store detective eyeing a couple of potential shoplifters. "So, are you saying you don't have an... understanding with anyone that could be construed as... an attachment?"

She gave my bicep a rather painful poke. "No, silly, the field is quite free. When did you want to go out?"

The plate of crostini slipped from my nerveless fingers and hit the floor with a crash! The old saying about no good deed going unpunished had risen up to bite me in the tender bits. My instinctive response at such moments of peril is to freeze and hope that the predator moves on to other game. I held my breath, unfocused my eyes and tried to fade into my surroundings. After what seemed like an eternity, I returned to the mortal plane to find Judy still looking at me expectantly. I abandoned all hope and swore to myself that if I managed to squeeze out of this predicament, I would never lift a finger to help another human being as long as I lived—even if I was to be boiled alive and served with a dollop of horseradish on the side.

TWO

This Dirigible is Awfully Crowded

I am aware that there is a certain type of low fellow who delights in conquest. To a cur like this any female is fair game—be she an old chum's sister or the betrothed of the local vicar. Judy, being both an employee and someone my best friend had courted in the moonlight, was absolutely out of bounds. I had, however, led the innocent lass into a misapprehension. To disabuse her would wound her deeply.

Rock, hard place. What was a fellow to do? I looked for Bentley, but he was at the other end of the cabin ironing T-shirts.

Judy was looking at me with concern. "Are you all right?"

"Me? Never better."

"You've dropped your crostini."

"What, that? Just a flourish—like smashing one's champagne glass in the fireplace after a stirring toast. Hola!"

I seized another plate and hurled it to the floor. It smashed in a most satisfying manner.

"Oh my!"

Cheeseworth's head popped up from behind a sofa. "I say, is this a thing? I'll play!" He merrily hurled his own plate to the floor.

Cook leaned out from the galley. "Stop that!"

Cheeseworth hung his head in shame. "Sowwy, Cook. I thought it was a thing."

Bentley distilled himself out of the ether. "May I retrieve your appetizers, Sir?"

"Bentley, yes! Thank you."

"Would you like a fresh plate?"

"No, no, that's quite enough crostini for one evening."

"Very good, Sir."

I turned to Judy, who had been watching me all this while with a mysterious smile on her lips. "What were we talking about?"

"You were asking me out."

"Oh! That! Well... Hmmm."

I found it devilishly hard to concentrate with her staring like that. If only she would glance at the scenery and give me a chance to marshal my thoughts...

She poked my bicep again. I would have a bruise there tomorrow. "Why don't we go for a drink after the conference wraps up?"

"Why indeed?"

"Good. It's a date."

I slumped in defeat. "Is it? I suppose... well, there it is."

She finally looked away, a touch too late to be of any use to me, and stared at Binky. He had picked up a magazine, which he was holding upside down, and his eyes were peeping at us over the top of it.

"Binky's acting odd."

"Odder than usual, you mean?"

"He keeps squinting at us. Did you two have a falling out?"

"Not yet, but soon. Perhaps I'd better go and talk to him."

"All right. See you later."

"Yes. Until later, then."

I walked over to Binky as slowly as I could without actually going backward.

He threw down the magazine and leaned in eagerly. "Well? What did she say?"

"She does not consider herself engaged. Quite the opposite."

He leaned back with a sigh. "That's a relief."

"Is it?"

"I'm not saying matrimony is out of the question, but there's much to be said for the thrill of the chase."

"Yes. As to that, you may have to run pretty fast to catch her. She's definitely on the move."

He stared at me uncomprehendingly. "What?"

"Look here, you know I'd never poach in another man's trout stream."

"What's a trout?"

"It was some sort of fish, I believe, but don't distract me."

"What are you saying?"

"I'm saying that through no fault of my own I find myself taking her out for drinks."

Binky began to quiver. He shakily pointed a finger at my nose. "Judas!"

"Now, now..."

"Brutus!"

"It wasn't my idea."

"Whose was it, then?"

"Hers, of course."

He laughed bitterly. "So, she's in love with you?"

"My God, I hope not."

"Not good enough for you?"

"Too good by half. Look, old spoon, I only want what's best for you."

"And you think that would be a life of chastity?"

This was all getting to be a little much. "It's your own fault. You made me speak to her."

He finally ran out of air and slumped into a chair. "She was the one. I see it now. I shall never love again."

"When you thought you were engaged to her you were wretched!"

"That was the old me—before suffering had made a man of me."

"I'll fix it. Just give me time and I'll douse the fire within her. I have a natural gift for dousing the fires within women as you know."

He stared into the distance with reddening eyes. "Too late. Too late. I shall die alone, friendless, riddled with disease... no one to mourn for me."

I could see he was pretty low. Something sparked in the old noodle and I knew just what to do.

"See here, let's get Bentley on the case."

His head whipped around and his shoulders straightened. "By Jove, you've finally come to your senses."

We made our way to the far end of the cabin where Bentley had finished with the T-shirts and was busily ironing dungarees. He looked up at us. "Is there something you require, Sir?"

"A little advice, Bentley."

"Of course, Sir." He set down the steam iron and regarded us gravely.

"It's of a romantic nature."

"I see."

"You know Judy?"

"I am acquainted with the young lady."

"Well, she's somehow gotten it into her head that I'm keen on her."

"And are you keen on her, Sir?"

"No! I mean, she's a blossom of womanhood, but it's Binky here who's pawing at the ground."

His gears whirled for a moment. "You wish to rebuff her."

"But gently."

Binky held up a warning finger. "You mustn't harm a hair on her head."

"Perhaps it would be best if the young lady rebuffed you instead."

I had to chuckle at his naivete. "That would be a dream come true, but how on earth would you achieve it? I mean, look at me. What woman in her right mind..."

"What a conceited prig you are. I'm every bit as desirable as you," sniffed Binky.

"Come, come, old hound. Compare our profiles."

"You're just rich. That's your only attraction."

"You're being rather wounding."

Bentley made a small harrumphing sound. "Perhaps we could deal with the problem at hand, Sir?"

"My word! Have you figured it out already?"

"Miss Judy is a young lady of high principles, I believe?"

Binky's eyes lit with a fervent glow. "She will not compromise on matters of social justice."

"She's rather a blister about it," I added, sotto voce.

"Then my suggestion is that you perform an act so egregious that her feelings toward you turn to anger and disappointment rather than affection."

I frowned. "That seems like hard cheese for me."

Binky rounded on me. "It's your fault. Why shouldn't you bear the consequences?"

"Again, I must point out..."

"Knave. Miscreant. Reprobate."

Bentley harrumphed for a second time. "Assigning blame is of no useful purpose, Sir."

"What do you suggest I do? Wear stripes with checks? Relieve babies of their candy?"

"Nothing suggests itself at the moment. Perhaps this upcoming conference will present an opportunity."

"We've got to work fast. I'm having drinks with her after."

"I shall be on the alert, Sir."

There was a sudden scream of brakes from the tarmac outside, followed by slamming doors and the thunder of feet on the airship's gangway.

"What on earth is that?"

The cabin door flew open and there stood Aunt Hypatia, Uncle Hugo and—her lace glove already hopelessly tangled in a palm plant—the gangly frame of Euphonia Gumboot. The blood froze in my veins.

"Aunt! Uncle! What are you all doing here?"

My aunt fixed me with a gorgon's glare. "I might ask you the same thing. One could almost suspect you of fleeing my soiree."

"What? Don't be silly."

"Where are you off to, then?"

"Oh... just taking a little spin around the Cotswolds, then back in plenty of time."

"Very well. We shall accompany you."

"But... that is... oh drat! To be perfectly truthful, Aunt, an important meeting in New York makes it impossible for me to attend your soiree. I'm dreadfully sorry."

She gave a self-satisfied sniff and adjusted the train of her gown.

"Don't give it a thought."

"Really?"

"When I learned of your plans, I canceled my soiree. We are quite free to accompany you to New York."

Well, this was a blow to the midsection as you can imagine. I turned to Binky, who was innocently staring at the ceiling. "Did you make a general announcement at the club?"

"I only told Cheeseworth."

Cheeseworth was helping himself to the stuffed mushrooms. "And you know me. A sealed cwypt."

"All is explained," I sighed. I must say—that Jean Valjean fellow thought he had it bad with Javert, but if he'd had Aunt Hypatia on his tail it would have been a much shorter book.

"Well... make yourselves comfortable, everyone. Have you brought your luggage?"

Uncle Hugo had been staring around the cabin estimating the value of its contents. "We have... and sufficient packaged food for the duration."

"That really wasn't necessary, Uncle. You can't light a fire to heat anything, you know. Hydrogen, apparently."

"Impossible Mutton can be eaten cold if one scrapes off the congealed gravy. I rather prefer it."

I could no longer ignore the vigorous pantomime taking place between Euphonia and the palm tree, which had taken hold of her glove with an unbreakable grip.

"And you've brought Euphonia!"

My aunt gazed on her struggles benevolently. "I promised her dinner and I am a person of my word."

Euphonia took a breather from her exertions. "I'm sorry, could someone detach me from this plant?"

Binky jogged eagerly toward her. "Here, let me."

"Thank you."

"Not at all. Oh! Now it's got me as well."

The buttons of his jacket had been happily seized by the playful palm. Euphonia stamped a surprisingly large foot.

"Plants are always attacking me. I don't see why we're always trying to save them."

Binky was concentrating fiercely on his buttons. "Neither do I. Lot of work, plants. Always needing water and whatnot. Like babies, aren't they?"

"Exactly. Yet when I suggest that we replace them with artificial copies I get the most censorious looks."

"Well, I'm in favor."

He gave the plant a vigorous shake and gazed at it thoughtfully. "Do you know, I think it will be easier to remove my jacket and just leave it hanging. Like fruit."

"And I shall do the same with my glove. What fun!"

They proceeded to divest themselves of the articles in question. My aunt glared.

"Does this play have an intermission? One would like to sit down."

I indicated a nearby chaise. "Yes, do sit down."

Aunt Hypatia has always been partial to Cheeseworth, who brought his mushrooms and sat beside her.

"Hello, Cheeseworth. Coming to New York, are you?"

"Hoping to relive old memories. I spent some years there working as a shoe shine boy to earn money for cigarettes after my father cast me from the bosom of my family."

Aunt Hypatia shook her head. "An unfortunate time."

"He was not a tolerant man and my love of musical comedy was the final stwaw. He is in a coma now and our welationship has impwoved."

Again, our peace was shattered by a squeal of tires.

"I wonder who that could be?"

A car door slammed, the gangway thundered and the door of the dirigible was hurled open once again. Cubby Martinez, the officious Marshall of Twits, stood panting at the entryway.

"Stop this dirigible!"

"Cubby?"

"The same!"

"What on earth are you doing here?"

"Protecting the honor of my family."

Euphonia stepped forward and thumped Cubby on the shoulder. "Oh Cubby, go away."

My head swam. "Euphonia? You know this man?"

"He is my stepbrother."

"What?"

"And I'll thank you to unhand my sister, Chippington-Smythe."

"I'm nowhere near your sister, physically or spiritually."

"There is a name for men who spirit innocent young ladies out of the country for who knows what immoral purpose."

Binky raised a hand. "Is it Raoul?"

"Look here, Cubby—I know we have our differences but on this subject we are united. Take your sister and depart. I will not lift a finger to stop you."

Bentley was suddenly at my elbow. "Pardon me, Sir, I'm afraid that is no longer possible. We have begun our ascent."

"Have we?"

"It has been a smooth departure."

I ran to a window and goggled at the receding firmament. "Well, Cubby old man, it looks like you're coming to New York with us."

"What? Turn this blimp around at once."

Bentley shook his head gravely. "I'm afraid that is impossible, Sir. There is a brisk westward wind that makes returning impractical."

My aunt gave a contented grunt. "All has worked out in a satisfactory manner. Euphonia now has a family member to chaperone her and no one can say we have not observed the proprieties."

Cubby's eyes began to redden. "But who will enforce the club rules? The members will run riot."

I shook my head. "You've no one to blame but yourself, Cubby. If you didn't have such an infernal heavy hand there wouldn't be all this pent-up pressure to act out."

"Any physical damage to the club will be on your head, Chippington-Smythe!"

I sighed. "You really are a pustule."

Cook appeared, wiping her hands with a striped towel. "Dinner will be ready in five minutes."

Thank you, Cook."

"There's gazpacho, focaccia and leeks vinaigrette with walnuts."

My mouth began to water. "Yum!"

Aunt Hypatia was unmoved. "Just put out some of the packaged dinners we brought and a pair of scissors. We can serve ourselves. We must practice living in a classless society if we are going to America."

Cook gave my aunt a hard stare and pressed her lips together until they turned white. "Yes, Ma'am."

As the company disposed themselves, my aunt moved inexorably toward me, forcing me to hop around various potted plants and ottomans until I found myself trapped in a corner. It seemed there was no escape. Like a choir director holding open calls for the Christmas Fete, I would be forced to face the music.

"Well, young man, you have caused me a great deal of inconvenience. What do you have to say for yourself?

And I may as well tell you that whatever you say I have already determined to disregard it."

"The truth is I couldn't stand another table full of prospective brides chewing and staring and simpering at me—especially the aptly named Miss Gumboot. It's more than flesh and blood can bear."

My aunt extracted a lace handkerchief from an invisible pocket and delicately blew her nose. "There is a simple solution."

"Which is?"

"Find an acceptable young lady and I shall no longer feel obliged to present you with the smorgasbord of femininity that you seem to detest so vigorously."

I spotted Judy heading our way and a light went on in the dusty attic just behind my forehead. "As it happens, Aunt, I have found just such a young lady."

She eyed me suspiciously. "Oh? I trust she is not in the theatrical profession. The family has been burned too many times by females of that ilk."

"Not at all. She's my head of Social Justice. A very intelligent young woman."

"I shall be the judge of that. I must assure myself that she is suitable. If not, Miss Gumboot remains within easy reach and can be proposed to with a minimum of preparation."

The unsuspecting Judy rolled up.

"Ah! Here she is! Judy, you remember my Aunt Hypatia?"

"Yes. Hello."

Judy presented a hand, which my aunt touched briefly with her fingertips.

"Your greeting is from the minimalist school. It reveals little. We must converse at greater length."

"You've met before you know, Aunt."

My aunt waved a hand. "When I encounter a person, I always assume that we have met before. It avoids much unpleasantness."

I turned to Judy. "I was just telling my aunt about us. You know... about us going for drinks... and the rest."

She looked at me oddly. "Oh. All right."

My aunt was staring at her through a small pair of glasses that she had produced from another pocket.

"You're quite a pretty thing. Your hips are rather narrow, but the babies in our family tend to be stunted."

Judy stared back at her. "Babies?"

"I am being premature... which is another characteristic of the family's offspring."

At that moment, thank heavens, Uncle Hugo called out from the dinner table, "Hypatia, would you prefer Chickeny Nuggets in a brown sauce or Implausible Ham in a yellow sauce?"

She bellowed back at him. "It makes little difference. They taste much the same." She turned to Judy. "Excuse me, my dear. My husband fancies himself a chef. If I do not intervene, he may attempt to improve my dinner by mixing the contents of various bags and adding quantities of salt to disastrous effect. I shall continue my interrogation at dinner."

She stomped off. "Stop what you are doing at once, Hugo, do you hear?"

Judy looked at me with her hands on her hips.

I smiled sheepishly. "Sorry about my aunt."

"What was all that about babies?"

I concentrated furiously. "I should have warned you—she's... eccentric. Never had children of her own and is obsessed with babies. Evaluates the fertility of every female she meets. Talks of nothing else. Just ignore her."

She glanced over at my aunt sympathetically. "Poor thing. Where are you sitting?"

I smiled winningly. "Next to you, of course. Save us a couple of seats."

"All right. Don't be too long."

"I caught Binky's eye and jerked my head in the general direction of a quiet corner. He looked at me uncomprehendingly.

"What are you doing?"

"Shh. Never mind. Come here!"

He strolled over. "What on earth is the matter?"

"I'm afraid something's come up and I can't give Judy the heave-ho just yet."

He stamped a hoof. "But you promised!"

"And I will honor that promise—after we return from America. For now, she is the only thing standing between me and the horrifying Miss Gumboot."

Binky looked over at the party in question and smiled. "Euphonia? I think she's charming."

I looked at him disbelievingly. "You really are the closest thing to a Bonobo."

"Of course she can't hold a candle to Judy. It's just that I appreciate her wit and good humor."

"Do you? Then do a chap a favor—use all of your animal magnetism to keep her off of me until I can kick her down the gangplank at the end of this adventure."

"What's in it for me?"

"Is friendship not enough?"

"No."

"Very well, what do you want?"

"I want that new tie you acquired from Borgen and Bots. The one with the palm tree on it."

"I love that tie!"

"Nevertheless."

I wriggled for a bit, but he had me by the ears and he knew it. "It's yours, you pirate."

Bentley wafted over. "Dinner, Sir."

"Look here, Bentley, there's been a change of plans. Until I am safely out of range of Miss Gumboot, I must maintain the ruse that Judy and I are engaged in a wild flirtation."

He fixed his optical sensors on me grimly. "It may make your ultimate aim of severing your connection with Miss Judy more complicated, Sir."

"It can't be helped. We must put out one fire at a time and Euphonia is a three-alarm flaming dumpster."

"I understand, Sir."

He paced away. Binky was eyeing me suspiciously. "It is only a ruse, isn't it? You're not trying to cut me out with Judy?"

"How can you say such a thing?"

He blushed with shame. "You're right. I'm acting like that Othello chap. Green-eyed muenster and all that.

"Monster!"

He looked injured. "What have I done now?"

I put a reassuring hand on his shoulder. "No. It's the green-eyed *monster*. Not muenster. Muenster was a cheese, I believe. Now come, they're waiting for us."

With a heart brimming with dread, I stalked toward the dinner table—a seething swamp populated with carnivorous predators in every direction... and gazpacho.

THREE

A Long Day's Journey to Manhattan

Dinner did not begin well. My aunt and her retinue sat at one end of the table, pouring turgid pools of neon-colored sauce from plastic packets onto their plates. As I approached the table, Euphonia waved at me gaily.

"Yoo-hoo, Cyril, sit here by me."

"I forbid it!"

Euphonia gave her brother a slap on the arm. "Shut up, Cubby."

Binky suavely inserted himself between them and slid into the vacant chair. "I'm afraid I must claim that seat for myself and reap the... plentiful bounty of your company in all its... autumnal splendor, Miss Gumboot."

She simpered at him. "Oh dear, that sounds gallant. Is it meant to be gallant?"

Binky frowned. "I believe so. I rather lost the thread about halfway through."

"I try never to utter a sentence of more than twelve words. It keeps me from losing my way quite so often." Uncle Hugo slid a plate over to her. She clapped her hands gaily. "Oh, I love implausible ham!"

Cheeseworth leaned over. "That was my review in the one foray into acting I attempted. The play was, 'Don't Just Stand There, Kill Something' and I was the lovesick gamekeeper. The Daily Snob called me 'an implausible ham.' I think I have the clipping about me somewhere."

He began rifling through pockets. I noticed that Cubby had refused the plate my uncle offered him.

"What will you have, Cubby? You're welcome to join us in sybaritic splendor as we revel in Cook's culinary genius."

"Nothing, thank you. Just a glass of water."

"Not hungry?"

"I will not dignify this kidnapping by eating the bread of my oppressors."

I sat back and regarded him with astonishment. "You know we'll be gone for days?"

"Nevertheless."

Binky shrugged. "You're made of sterner stuff than I, Cubby. I get woozy if I go more than two hours without a snack."

"And I suppose you're proud of that. All you elites are the same."

My uncle pointed a fork at Cubby. "Steady on, Sir."

"You've never known want. You've never gone a day without food."

I gazed at him in astonishment. "Have *you*?"

"I won't dignify that with a reply."

Euphonia looked up from her "ham". "Cubby was dreadfully poor as a child."

"That's enough, Euphonia!"

"His father was a scoundrel. Gambled everything away. It wasn't until our mother remarried my father that the family fortunes improved."

"I forbid you to say another word!"

Aunt Hypatia looked thoughtful. "I knew your father, Mr. Martinez. He led your poor mother a merry dance. I used to send her my old garments or she would have gone about looking like a scarecrow."

"This is excruciating! Please change the subject."

"It's nothing to be ashamed of," Binky gargled around a mouthful of leeks vinaigrette. "I've barely got two pennies to rub together."

Cubby sneered. "But you will never be thrown into the street. You have friends and relations who will always support you."

"Have you no friends?"

"I do not need or wish for friendship. I have my duty and that is enough. Now I insist that we speak no more of this."

As the host, the onus was on me to change the subject. "Let's turn our attention to this delightful dinner. *Bon appetit*, everyone."

Euphonia, who apparently didn't speak French, looked alarmed. "Are there bones in it? I hope I don't choke."

Binky winked at her coquettishly. "Would you like me to cut it into little pieces for you?"

"Would you? How chivalrous."

Binky went to work with the knife and fork, but his attention was focused on Miss Gumboot rather than the slippery slices of "ham," and a large chunk flew off the plate in Cubby's direction.

"Careful, you clod! I don't have a change of clothing."

"Slippery little devils," said Binky.

Euphonia smiled at him. "It's the sauce. It is oleaginous."

"What a spiffing word!"

"It is one of my favorites. I have far too few occasions to use it." She drew the word out languorously. "Oleaginous."

Binky reddened. "You are naughty, Miss Gumboot."

I nipped this flirtation in the bud. "Have you been to New York, Aunt?"

"Never. Travel is broadening, they say, and that is never a good thing."

"What about you, Uncle Hugo?"

"Heavens no. It is a savage place, by all accounts. We have business in America, but it is accomplished through the mail."

"I've heard New York is thrilling."

Aunt Hypatia shook her head grimly. "You prove my point. Being thrilled is cousin to being hysterical. They both involve adrenaline, which is the most uncouth of all the hormones." My aunt set down her fork and turned the full force of her regard on Judy. "Now, my dear, tell me about yourself. Who are your people?"

I could see Judy's hackles rising. "My... people?"

"What is your parentage? From whom do you derive? Are there any hereditary flaws in your gene pool or institutionalized madmen we should be aware of?"

"What?!"

"Aunt! Let's not give her the third degree!"

Euphonia turned to Binky. "I've always wondered what the first two degrees are?"

"By Jove, that's a thought. I have a degree in something from University. It's either for history or cricket. I can't remember which."

Cook brought a huge platter and set it down in front of Judy. She stood staring at Aunt Hypatia with her fists on her hips. Judy took one of her hands. "Well, as far as my parentage is concerned, my mother is currently serving us this delicious focaccia, which you seem determined not to try."

My aunt was unperturbed. "You mustn't take it personally, Cook. My digestive system is extremely delicate. So, your people are in service?"

Judy grew redder. "Is there anything wrong with that?"

"No, no. I think at least one person in a relationship should know how to light a fire or apply a tourniquet. We may not always be able to rely on civilization. How many children do you intend to produce?"

I gave Judy a significant glance. Her irritation changed at once to solicitude as she leaned toward my aunt.

"I'm sorry you were never able to have children of your own. Was it a medical problem?"

My aunt was taken aback. "Of course not. I am physically perfect in every respect."

"Then was it your husband?"

Hugo looked up from his plate. "I beg your pardon?"

"He too is, if not exceptional, then at least average in every way. It was the combination that proved toxic. My theory is that Hugo's sperm were so boring that my eggs simply went into hibernation."

My uncle threw down his fork. "This is hardly dinner table conversation."

"I have yet to find a subject that you find acceptable at table. Why masticating food should require such curated content I will never understand. Now, Jerry..."

"Judy."

"Indeed? I was sure it was Jerry."

"No."

"You could easily change it."

"I am fond of my name."

"Are you? Oh well. Back to the matter of children, as in, quantity of?"

"One or two, I suppose. I haven't given it a lot of thought."

"Two should be the minimum requirement. Siblings are the fiery crucible that smelts out the essence of our character. I had a brother and it was invaluable."

"Where is he now?"

"I have no idea. He stopped speaking altogether at the age of ten and began haunting public libraries. That was the last I heard of him."

"Poor thing."

"There are instances of one twin consuming the other in the womb. We were not twins but it was much the same thing."

Cheeseworth dabbed his lips with his napkin. "How I longed for a sibling. My father's member was lost in an incident involving a pwinting pwess and that was that. I was a lonely child, which I think explains my obsession with puppets."

Binky tore his gaze away from Euphonia and looked around the cabin. "I say, it's getting rather dark. One can barely discern where one's plate leaves off and the tablecloth begins. Couldn't we have some light?"

My uncle shook his head. "I'm afraid not. The nearness of the hydrogen makes lamps far too dangerous."

Euphonia gave a start. "Oh! I believe I've eaten my powder puff."

"Are you all right?"

She smiled at Binky. "Yes. Actually, it soaked up the sauce admirably."

Binky simpered. "The oleaginous sauce?"

She gave a little shriek and punched him in the arm. "La, Mr. Wickford-Davies, what a rake you are."

Cubby glared at Binky. "I trust you are not taking advantage of this darkness to play patty-cake with my sister."

Euphonia raised her fork. "Is there cake? I'll have a slice."

I threw up my hands. "Well, this is impossible. Darkness has come like a thief in the night. What on Earth shall we do now?"

My aunt huffed. "Whenever I find myself in an impossible situation I simply go to bed. That is the answer to most of life's conundrums."

"But how to find our beds? I can't see my hand in front of my face."

Bentley appeared at my elbow. "Pardon me, Sir. My sensors are unaffected by darkness. I shall guide you to your sleeping compartments one at a time."

"Excellent. While I'm waiting for my turn, just put a slice of focaccia in the old mitt, would you?"

"Of course, Sir."

Eventually, Bentley led me to my little sleeping cabin and in no time, I was snoring away and dreaming of pancakes.

I woke with the light streaming in and a moist mouthful of pillow. There was just time for a brush-up and a bite of a cold breakfast before we touched down and began unloading.

"This is the way to travel, eh, Binky?"

"According to the Captain we broke all records for an Atlantic crossing. Apparently, the wind was up our tails."

"I think that's called a tail wind, old mouse."

"I say, could I have a little word?"

"Of course, my lad. We are as brothers. Step this way."

We strolled to a pile of rusty old barrels. Binky cleared his throat. "The thing is... I don't know how much longer I can keep this up. Flirting with Miss Gumboot is exhausting and we didn't figure Cubby into the equation."

"You must not flag nor weaken. I need you to be a shield unto my right arm against the forces of Euphonia Gumboot for the weekend."

"All right, but one tie is not enough. I want a bottle of that cologne you drench yourself in."

"You mean 'Insouciance'? Fine. Done."

"And when you are ready to give Judy the heave-ho, I want to be nearby so that I can catch her on the short hop."

"You really are an excrescence and a plague."

"Wait until you fall in love. No power on earth can stay its course."

"My fondest wish is that you marry Judy and have plentiful offspring. That will be revenge enough for me."

"I knew you'd understand."

I looked around at the general decay. "I say, where are we? Rather dismal."

Bentley glided over as if he were on skates. "New Jersey, Sir. There is no closer airfield that can accommodate dirigibles of this size."

At that moment I noticed a rather disheveled looking fellow leaning against the car. He was trying to dislodge something from between his teeth with a toothpick and was eyeing the dirigible. He saw me looking at him and redoubled his efforts with the toothpick. A badge affixed to his greasy lapel suggested that he was the customs inspector.

"That your blimp?"

"It is."

"You can't leave it there, you know."

"I can hardly do anything else with it."

He shifted the toothpick. "I guess I could take care of it for you."

"Could you? That's awfully decent of you."

"Course it'll cost you."

"How much?"

He switched the toothpick to another gap in his teeth and wrinkled his forehead. "It's usually five hundred."

I turned to Bentley in shock. "Bentley?"

"I believe a bribe is customary, Sir."

"Is it a bribe?"

"I believe so."

"It seems like a lot."

The customs inspector sighed. "Course I could write you up a ticket. You could go down to the courthouse and pay a fine. Shouldn't take you more than eight or nine hours."

"Look here, my dear sir, I'm not accustomed to paying blackmail."

"Ain'tcha?"

"No, I am not."

He spat out the toothpick. "Welcome to Jersey."

Bentley stepped between us. "It's quite all right, Sir. I shall see to it. Why don't you make yourself comfortable in the automobile."

"All right. Get in, everyone. I'm dying for a proper wash up and some hot food."

We wedged ourselves into the automobile. As ill fortune would have it, I wound up next to Cubby. He looked around sourly. "Does anyone have a spare toothbrush? I came with nothing."

"We come into this world with nothing and depart with nothing," I chirped.

"But while we're here, a toothbrush is not an unreasonable request."

Bentley slid into the driver's seat. "I shall procure one when we reach the hotel, Sir."

I leaned away from Cubby. "Until then could you roll down a window, old sock? There's a distinct aroma of low tide."

"Laugh now, Chippington-Smythe. There shall come a day of reckoning."

The hotel was a grand old thing. We swept into the lobby only to be halted by an officious young person with a clipboard and pen.

"Excuse me, Sir, before you check in, I just have a few questions for you."

"Do you need to see my passport? Bentley has all that."

"No, Sir. This will only take a moment."

"Fire away."

She consulted her clipboard. "Green or blue?"

"Green or blue what?"

"Which is your favorite?"

"I suppose... green. No, blue!"

My aunt gave a grunt. "The correct answer should be gold, but apparently that is not an option."

The young lady made a little check on her clipboard. "Eight planets or nine?"

"I beg your pardon?"

"Scientists recently reclassified Pluto as a planetoid instead of a planet. Do you accept that there are only eight planets in our solar system or do you believe there are still nine?"

"I'm the last person to ask about science. Only last week Bentley had to explain to me how elastic works. Damned useful for keeping one's socks up, it turns out."

"Planets, Sir?"

"Well... eight, I suppose."

My aunt shook her head. "What does it matter how many there are? It is enough for a person of quality to know that planets exist. Counting them is the work of mathematicians or public accountants."

"The tomato: fruit or vegetable?"

Cheeseworth tapped his jeweled walking stick on the tile floor. "That's a twick question. Tomato is a paste, as everyone knows."

"This is becoming far too personal," huffed my aunt. "You Americans should learn that sharing one's innermost thoughts will drive away all but the most undesirable company."

Uncle Hugo could take no more. "What do these questions have to do with checking into this establishment?"

The young lady looked up from her clipboard. "Nothing, Sir."

I stared at her in amazement. "Do you not work for the hotel?"

"No, Sir."

My aunt gazed at her shrewdly. "Young lady, you have taken advantage of our credulity to winkle out our most intimate beliefs. I am impressed."

"Your input is invaluable. Social media could not exist without it."

"Well, really! Come on, everyone."

The desk clerk was vaguely reminiscent of the steam-powered servants that populated Twits. I suppose there was a generic type of automaton that was pumped out by the thousands all over the world. We did the necessary and I took the offered key.

"Could someone take the bags up to our room?"

The desk clerk looked at me solemnly. "We no longer provide that service, Sir."

"What? Why not?"

"The bell persons tried to unionize, and we were forced to eliminate them."

I stared at him helplessly. "How do we get all of this luggage upstairs?"

"Not to worry, Sir." He clanged a hand bell and focused his eyes into the middle distance. "This gentleman needs his bags taken to his room. The hotel takes no responsibility either legal or moral for any paid employment that might result from this situation."

A small mob of hungry-looking individuals suddenly appeared from the shadows.

"Carry your bags, Mister? Dollar a bag?"

Another ragged-looking fellow straightened the bit of string that stood in for a tie. "I'll do it for seventy-five cents a bag, Sir."

The first would-be porter gave him a shove. "You don't want him. Leper. Likely to lose a finger and come after you for medical bills."

"That's a lie! He's got fleas."

"I don't!"

As they argued, a third gentleman simply placed our bags on a wheeled cart and headed for the elevator. We quietly slipped away and followed him. As the doors slid closed the first two fellows were still arguing.

"Bit of a thicket, this dog-eat-dog economy."

The fellow with our bags sighed deeply. "It is, Sir. It is an affront to the dignity of man."

"You're very well spoken for a bellman."

"I used to be a teacher."

"What made you give it up?"

He looked down sadly. "I taught penmanship. When they banned cursive writing I could no longer find employment."

We arrived at my room. I opened the door and he tossed in the bags.

"This is your room. If there's anything you need, just go to the lobby and shout. Who's next?"

He wandered off with the rest of our party trailing behind him... all but Binky, who slipped into my room before I could close the door.

"Do you mind if I lounge about here for a while? I hate being alone in hotel rooms. I can't flush the loo because they've put that blue solution in it and I don't like to disturb it."

"Consider this your second home."

Bentley condensed out of thin air. "Yes, Bentley?"

"A gentleman is here to see you."

"Did he give his name?"

"He did not, Sir. He states that he is known popularly as the Social Media King."

"Wasn't the whole point of America to do away with Kings?"

"Perhaps the title is ironic, Sir."

"Yoiks! Irony is like a pink marshmallow. It promises delight but cloys after the first nibble. Show him in."

Bentley evaporated toward the door and soon returned with the gentleman in question. "The Social Media King, Sir."

Had I been one of those prognosticators who can pierce the veil of time and see into the future I would have done my best to stifle the fellow with a pillow at once, but alas, the flow of time carries us all inexorably toward the cataracts of our doom.

Four

The Pirate King

The King was a thin young man with strikingly long arms and fingers. His eyes maintained a fixed stare which was made more unnerving by a complete absence of blinking. I stuck out the old paw.

"Hallo. Cyril Chippington-Smythe. This is my boon companion, Cheswick Wickford-Davies, but everyone calls him Binky. Here for the conference, are you? I'm simply champing at the bit to wade into all that science and whatnot. Care for a drink?"

"I don't drink alcohol. Um... It slows your mental processes."

"Quite right. Nothing for me as well."

I slid my brandy and soda behind a nearby lamp.

"I hope you don't mind that I came to your room. Um... I wanted to talk to you privately."

Binky leaned toward the door. "Should I go?"

I seized him by the sleeve. "Certainly not. You are a trusted confidante."

The Social Media King eyed him dubiously. "Can he keep a secret?"

"Don't worry," I assured him, "whatever he remembers will be so garbled as to be unintelligible."

Binky gave a little bow. "Thank you very much."

I gestured to the seating area. "Let's park ourselves in these comfy-looking armchairs and have a good chin wag."

"If you don't mind, um, I haven't reached my daily step count, so I'll just..."

He began marching in place. Good manners seemed to dictate that we join him. We faced each other and jerked our knees up and down like wind-up tin soldiers.

Binky began to trip over his feet at once. "I don't think I'm doing it right. Is there a hop somewhere in the pattern?"

"It's just left, right, left, right, etcetera, old boot."

We settled into an easy rhythm and waited for the Social Media King, who I will refer to hereafter as the SMK, to begin.

"The thing is, I represent a group of individuals who prefer to remain anonymous."

Binky frowned. "Then how do you contact them?"

"They're not anonymous to me."

"They're not very good at it then, are they?"

The SMK shook his head and decided to ignore Binky, which showed some discernment on his part, I must say.

"This group I represent is pretty powerful. It shapes, um, public opinion on everything from fashion to politics."

I giggled nervously. "Goodness, it almost sounds like you're part of a secret cabal hiding in the shadows and pulling the strings while the world's governing bodies dance like puppets."

This seemed to alarm him. "There isn't any such cabal and if there were, like you said, um... it would be a secret."

I eyed him thoughtfully. "So if it existed, you would be forced to deny its existence."

"Right."

"Then your denial that it exists is proof that it does, in fact, exist!"

"It doesn't exist."

"So you're saying that it does exist."

Binky gave up marching and glared at us both. "Could you at least wink or waggle your eyebrows? I'm getting a headache."

"Um, has anyone approached you since you got here with a survey?"

"Yes. In the lobby."

"They work for me. I have an army of people that go everywhere, um, surveying the population about their opinions."

"To what end?"

"To find controversy. There are a huge number of issues that divide us."

"Just so. My club, 'Twits,' is divided between the 'Neat' and the 'With ice' factions that will never be reconciled."

"Right. So we've found out if you make people angry enough, they'll buy whatever you're selling."

I frowned at him. "It doesn't seem like that's improving anyone's life."

"Well, if by 'life' you mean a dull, gray slog where every day is just like the one before it: working, eating, sleeping and dying... then we give people excitement, a rush of adrenaline, um... passion!"

"When you put it like that..."

"People want to fight for a cause, even if it's petty. They want to believe in something, um, even if it's absurd."

Binky's eyes grew large. "It's like you're describing my whole life!"

"But what do you want with me?"

He slowed his jog to a walk. "We want to make you a partner."

Binky looked disgusted. "Him? A member of a cabal? Some fellows have all the luck. Secret handshake, I shouldn't wonder. Key chain with a mysterious medallion, one expects."

The SMK looked at me. "We have all of that and more. What about it?"

"Oh. Well, of course I can't say off the top of my head... complicated web of investments and all that. Why do you need a partner? You seem to be doing well."

"We're expanding into the overseas market. You have an army of hydrogen meter readers that go door to door and apparently your government has made it a crime to shut the door on them. They could carry my surveys with them on their rounds. I'd get my data and you'd make millions."

My mind began to buzz. "Do you know... I'll have to think it over for a bit, but it's damned exciting."

The squeaking of cart wheels announced the entrance of Cook, pushing a tiny trolley with a soup tureen and bowls. "Here we go. Cock-a-leekie soup with some lovely croutons."

Binky made a beeline for her. "Goodie!"

"Ah! Cook. Well, I suppose I'll have to stop marching if I'm going to eat hot soup. Self-preservation, you know."

The SMK ignored Cook completely and sped up to a jog again. "I'll keep going, if that's okay."

Cook smiled at him as if he were a benign lunatic. "Would your guest care for a wee bowl of soup?"

He glanced over. "Who makes it?"

She drew herself up indignantly. "I make it. Who else?"

"It's not from a factory?"

"You won't find anything from a factory in my kitchen."

He came jogging over. "Okay. I'll try it."

Cook ladled him out a bowl. He managed to get a spoonful into his mouth without slowing. "Um... that's... wow! That's good!"

I was accustomed to this reaction when people tasted Cook's food. I myself had once been rendered speechless by a cherry clafoutis, and on another occasion had to be revived after a particularly savory roasted cauliflower with sauce romesco. The SMK looked at me with newfound respect.

"You eat like this all the time?"

"I have canceled luxurious trips to exotic locales because Cook could not accompany me."

Cook smacked me on the arm. "You're laying it on with a trowel. Eat your soup and I'll bring you a nice treacle tart."

"My favorite!"

Cook squeaked away. There was a knock at the door, which flew open to reveal my aunt and Euphonia, who was dressed in an eccentric outfit that seemed to have been assembled at a military surplus store. "Is that what you're wearing to the conference, Euphonia?"

"I was told to avoid fashion at all costs."

She had succeeded admirably. I brought forth the SMK. "May I present the Social Media King. This is my Aunt Hypatia and Miss Euphonia Gumboot."

He continued shoveling soup into his cake hole. "Hello."

Euphonia made a staggering lurch. "Your highness."

"Um... you don't have to bow."

"To be truthful I didn't intend to bow. I lost my balance."

Binky smiled at her shyly. "Hallo, Euphonia."

"Hello... I'm sorry, I've forgotten your name."

"What?"

"I do remember your face."

Binky looked forlorn. "Binky. My name is Binky."

"Is it? How odd."

My aunt was examining the SMK approvingly. "Nephew, I am happy to see that you are associating with a rarefied class of people. Over which kingdom do you rule, Your Highness?"

"So... I'm not an actual king."

Her face fell. "Then you should not call yourself one. If people give themselves titles will you nill you, they will soon lose all meaning, and drawing up a seating chart for dinner will become impossible."

"Well, it's the only name I use. I have to protect my anonymity."

"Anonymity is greatly over-rated... and leads to very few invitations."

Euphonia had been staring vacantly about the room but this seemed to perk her up. "I was Anonymous once, but I missed having wine with dinner."

The SMK seemed to notice her for the first time. "That's good. You're funny."

"That's what my father always said. 'There's something funny about you, Euphonia.' He used to squint at me in the oddest way when he said it."

"Are you here for the conference too?"

"Oh no. I only came for dinner. There have been several other meals as well, fortunately. Dinner was quite some time ago and I am susceptible to hypoglycemia."

The SMK gave a barking laugh. "Is she for real?"

My aunt regarded Euphonia grimly. "She gives every indication of being real. The food must go somewhere."

Euphonia suddenly jerked her head to one side and gave a little hop. "Oh dear, my hair has gotten tangled in these parachute clips."

Aunt Hypatia took her arm. "Come into the other room with me, my dear. If I cannot untangle it, I shall find a pair of scissors. I have always thought that your hair expressed itself too freely. Excuse us for a moment."

She led Euphonia away. The SMK watched them go with a calculating look on his face then turned to me. "Um... I have the contracts in my room. Why don't I go and bring them back for you to take a look at?"

"Jolly good."

"I'll just be a minute."

He jogged out of the room, still holding the soup bowl. As the door closed behind him Binky turned to me.

"Are you going to join the cabal, you lucky brute?"

"I don't know. I say, Bentley?"

He had been there the whole time, of course, but had made himself invisible in that way he had.

"Sir?"

"Did you overhear our conversation?"

"Yes, Sir."

"What do you think of his proposal?"

Bentley's optical sensors vibrated for a moment and I heard a grinding sound from his cranium. "I believe he is correct in his assessment of your potential profits, Sir. It seems a lucrative venture."

"Wouldn't Uncle Hugo be agog?"

"He would indeed, Sir."

I didn't care about the money, of course—I rolled about in filthy lucre day and night. No, what excited me was the thought of doing it on my own. No Uncle Hugo or Board of Directors to make the decisions for me. I saw myself swaggering into the club and casually remarking, "Started a new business this week. Did it all on my own. No help from anyone. Bringing in a million a day. Anyone for tennis?" By Jove, it made the old blood rather sing in one's veins. I heard a strange, gurgling sound.

"Have you finished pouring your cock-a-leekie soup on the carpet, Sir?"

I snapped out of it to find Bentley looking at the floor sadly. "What? Damn! Forgot I was holding it."

"Quite understandable. I shall procure a mop."

Binky looked at his own bowl of soup. "Should I pour mine on the carpet as well? No, it's too tasty. I'm going to finish it."

The door flew open to admit Uncle Hugo and Cheeseworth. Cheeseworth was dressed in a dirty apron and wrinkled work pants.

"My old shoe shine uniform! I've kept it all these years as a memento and it still fits! I could go right back to work polishing boots."

"A brutal profession. You must have spent hours down on your knees."

"Still do, dear boy, still do."

My uncle had clearly attempted to go native. His torso strained to escape the flimsy T-shirt that confined it. "By Jove, these T-shirts rival anything Torquemada could have imagined."

Aunt Hypatia re-entered the room leading Euphonia, whose hair was noticeably shorter.

"Is that you whining, Hugo?"

"I was not whining."

Cheeseworth stared down at the rug. "This pool of soup on the carpet hints at a tale of violence and intwigue."

"Just clumsiness I'm afraid."

Bentley returned with a mop and bucket. "If you would be so good as to step to the left, I will clean it up in a trice."

"My left or your left?"

"Either would be thrilling, Sir."

Uncle Hugo fell into an armchair. "These Americans are a warlike tribe. The chambermaid asked me how many planets there are and when I said 'nine' she hurled a bar of soap at my head."

"Passions are running high," I agreed.

At that moment the SMK returned. He had changed for the conference and wore a polo shirt in a blue-green color I would describe as teal. He bore a thick sheaf of papers. He stopped upon seeing the crowd.

"Hello."

"May I present the Social Media King? King, this is my uncle, Hugo Dankworth and C. Langford-Cheeseworth."

He nodded at them. "Glad to meet you."

My uncle had jumped from his chair upon hearing the word "King."

"Are you here for the conference as well, Your Highness?"

My aunt shook her head. "'King' is more aspirational than actual, Hugo. I shall explain later."

I caught the King's eye and jerked my head toward a quiet corner. He and I crept away from the crowd.

"Let's keep our little business arrangement between us for the time being, shall we? Loose lips and all that," I murmured quietly.

"Sure, if that's what you want. Here's the contract."

He handed me a stack of papers. I set them on a nearby table. "I'll just set it here by the sofa until later."

He pulled out another sheet. "And here's the latest social media release. There's a bunch of posts in there about you and your friends."

I looked at him in surprise. "How can that be?"

"My people are everywhere, recording people's reactions to everything. We type up the results all day long and distribute them by hand."

I took the sheet of paper and scanned it. "'The well-known society boob Cyril Chippington-Smythe arrived in New York today dressed like a cross between Louis *Quatorz* and a circus clown.' I say! 'He was in the company of Miss Euphonia Gumboot, social influencer and heiress to the Gumboot fortune. Are wedding bells in the offing?' This does cross the line!"

He looked at me eagerly. "You can respond if you want. It would be on the street in less than an hour."

I sniffed. "No thank you. Such things are beneath me."

"Everyone thinks that at first. You'll catch on. It's fun."

My uncle began pulling at his clothes. "This T-shirt is driving me mad! Local customs be damned, I'm going to change! Don't wait for me, Hypatia."

"The thought never crossed my mind."

I rejoined the company. "But Uncle, won't you miss the presentations?"

The SMK was right behind me. "No one listens to those. It's just an excuse to socialize. It's kind of lonely, being a tycoon. Most of them will be in the ballroom getting hammered."

Euphonia perked up. "That sounds lovely. Let's go there immediately!"

My aunt seated herself. "In a moment. I refuse to be on time for Americans."

The SMK gave a little bow. "I'd be happy to escort Miss Gumboot downstairs."

"Goodie! Let's go."

I waved them toward the door. "We'll only be a few minutes. I have to finish applying sweat stains to my clothing."

"Don't worry about me. The King will keep me company."

As he and Euphonia opened the door, Judy entered, squeezing past them. "Oh! Excuse me."

The SMK nodded his head at her. "We were just leaving."

Euphonia put her head on one side and stared at Judy. "You look familiar."

"We rode over on the dirigible together."

"Did we? Such fun. Ta-ta. See you at the party."

Judy watched them go and shook her head. "What an odd woman she is."

"Hello Judy," I chirped. She looked my outfit over.

"You look very... proletariat."

"I am *comme il faut*," according to Bentley."

Binky's eyes bored into her like a weevil into a cotton ball. "Hallo, Judy."

"Hi, Binky, you've got treacle tart on your shirt."

He brushed ineffectually at his clothing. "Do I? Damn. You could have said something, Cyril."

"I have a lot on my plate right now, old man."

Judy's gaze was disturbingly proprietary. "Cyril, I've been thinking."

This did not bode well. "Have you? Double-edged sword—thinking."

"Despite your outgoing exterior you're really very shy, aren't you?"

My aunt looked thoughtful. "I have always suspected something more pathological. 'Shy' seems almost a virtue by comparison."

"Perhaps I am protective of my more intimate feelings. What is your point?"

"You need to let yourself go a little. We're only young once, you know. You don't want to wither on the vine."

My aunt nodded. "An apt metaphor. One should experience life while one is still bursting with juice like a ripe grape. The wrinkled raisin of maturity arrives all too soon."

"So, I'm going to take you in hand," Judy concluded.

They say at the last moment of life one sees the entire landscape of one's journey pass by the old peepers. The prospect of being "taken in hand" apparently tripped the projector and scenes from childhood rose up before me: Bentley spooning Pablum into my tiny maw; Bentley teaching me to tie a proper bow tie; Bentley telling me how babies come about. That same Bentley now broke into my reverie by clearing his throat.

"The conference is about to begin, Sir. You wouldn't want to be tardy."

My aunt rose to her feet. "Come, Judy my dear. I will regale you with tales of Cyril as a child. They will not reflect well on him, but you should know what you are getting."

There was a pounding of heels in the hallway and the door burst open to admit a panting Cubby Martinez. He stared around the room with wild eyes and took a threatening step in my direction. "Where is my sister?!"

"Steady, Cubby. What's the ruckus?"

He pointed an accusing finger in my face. "Her bag is gone and she left a note saying that she refuses to return home."

"What?"

My aunt shook her head disapprovingly. "Rash child! Her reputation was already teetering on a knife's edge."

Cubby came a step closer. Fasting had not improved his breath, I must say. "What have you done with her, Chippington-Smythe?"

"Me? Nothing."

My Uncle Hugo stood up. "She left here with the Social Media King a few moments ago. They were going to the ballroom."

"Come on! We'll help you find her!"

I headed for the door. Binky followed close behind me. "It's like a game of hide and seek."

This caused Cubby to erupt. "It's not a game! Euphonia can't be left by herself. She lacks a short-term memory."

I stared at him. "What? Is that why she didn't remember me just now?"

Binky's eyes were round. "Nor me? She forgot my name."

Cubby stamped a foot. "She's got to be found at once!"

My aunt drew herself erect. "Come, everyone! To the ballroom."

Uncle Hugo waved at her. "Go without me. I must change my shirt."

She looked at him indulgently. "Yes, Hugo. When I refer to 'everyone,' I seldom include you."

"To the elevator!" I cried.

We piled into the elevator and I mashed the button. The elevator did not share our sense of urgency and drifted lazily down through the various floors, stopping at random and opening its doors on empty hallways. The entire ride was accompanied by some sort of syrupy orchestral arrangement that might have been "April in Paris" or could as easily have been "Beethoven's Fifth."

At long last we reached the ballroom level and rushed out to behold a seething mass of what were billed as "Titans of Industry." Most were dressed, like me, as if they had plans to paint their apartment later on. I turned to the group of hunters.

"Let's split up. Whoever spots them, give a yell."

We wove our way into the crowd like a pack of questing ferrets. I soon spied the wayward couple. They saw me at the same moment. The King grabbed Euphonia's hand and began pulling her in the opposite direction. So he was a party to her mad dash! I fought to reach them but the tide of humanity was too much for my sylphlike frame. I looked around me, saw a table covered with champagne glasses and swept them to the floor! Climbing gingerly onto the table I scanned the room. There they were, approaching the exit! Thinking quickly, I grabbed one of the remaining glasses and rapped on it loudly with a spoon. The noise abated somewhat.

"I say! Excuse me, ladies and gentlemen! May I have your attention please? There is an abduction in progress! That man there! In the blue polo shirt! Seize him!"

The crowd looked around in confusion. A gentleman near the SMK squinted at him and turned to shout at me.

"Who, this fellow? That's a green shirt."

His neighbor gave a disgusted grunt. "It is not. That's blue!"

"You're color blind. It's green."

This was getting us nowhere. I waved at them desperately. "All right then, teal! The man in the teal shirt!"

The second man put his hands on his hips and stared at me truculently. "Teal *is* blue."

"The hell it is! It's green!"

"Says who?"

"Says me!"

The rest of the crowd was starting to get interested.

"Sock him in the eye!"

"I'd like to see you try."

"Oh, you would, would you?"

I was practically wringing my hands. "Gentlemen and ladies, we are missing the point! The rotter is getting away!"

Alas, a punch was thrown and in an instant the room erupted into chaos. Screams of "Green!" and "Blue!" echoed amidst the stately columns. Champagne bottles arced lazily through the air. I saw my aunt fighting her way toward me with a terrifying singleness of purpose. Those in her way found themselves clubbed to the side by her capacious handbag. She waved urgently at me.

"Nephew! We must evacuate at once! The colonialists are revolting!"

In another part of the chamber a drunken reveler held Binky in a headlock while a shriveled nabob kicked him repeatedly in the derrière. Cheeseworth was struck in the midsection by a brutal slab of a man. He threw down his cane and delivered two sharp lefts and a right to the fellow's face, dropping him like a fallen tree... and as I watched helplessly Euphonia and the Social Media King calmly walked through the exit door and disappeared. Judy suddenly appeared next to me and held out a hand.

"Come on, Cyril. Let's get you out of here."

"Judy! They went that way!"

She nodded, grabbed my hand and hacked her way through the wall of human flesh. We flew out of the exit door and spotted the fugitives standing at the curb attempting to hail a cab.

"Halt! Not another step!"

The SMK looked at me nervously and held up a hand. "Okay, it's not what you think."

"It seldom is."

The exit door crashed open again and a discombobulated Cubby flew into our midst. He took in the situation at once and held out his perspiring hands to his stepsister. "Euphonia! How could you?"

"How could I what, Cubby?"

"How could you run off with this man? A virtual stranger."

"We're not running off. We're going to his office to sign a contract."

Cubby looked stunned. "A what?"

"The King has offered me a job."

"Doing what?"

Euphonia waved her hand gaily. "I'm to just say whatever comes into my head and someone will write it down for publication. He says it will drive people absolutely mad."

The SMK looked at her shyly. "She's phenomenal. No filter at all! Social media will love her!"

Cubby looked lost. "This can't really be what you want, Euphonia."

She looked at him kindly. "Yes, Cubby. You know I'm rather a joke back home. People snicker at me behind my back... I know they do. It's different in America. Here everyone lacks a short-term memory. I fit right in."

Cubby drew himself up. "I refuse. You do not have my permission."

"I do not need your permission. I am of age."

He slumped. "What if you are unhappy?"

"There is ample transportation between America and home, I believe. I shall simply buy a ticket."

Cubby looked at her helplessly. "Can this really be goodbye?"

"Yes. Goodbye Cubby."

I stepped forward. "Farewell, Euphonia."

She looked at me vaguely. "And who are you?"

"I'm Cyril. We've met."

"Oh, I don't think so."

Judy gave me a poke in the side. "Perhaps we shouldn't press the point."

I gave a little bow. "I hope, Euphonia, that being famous does not shatter the protective barrier between you and comprehension."

She paused for a moment. "What?"

"So far, so good."

A taxi pulled up, The King helped Euphonia into it and they sped off into the night. We stood and watched them disappear around a corner. Cubby spun toward me.

"This is your fault, Chippington-Smythe!"

"Mine? How?"

"You brought her to America."

"It was my aunt who brought her. It just happened to be my dirigible."

Cubby sneered. "That's right. You have a dirigible. I suppose that makes you better than me."

I sighed. "You really are exhausting."

Judy patted his arm. "Have you still not eaten anything, Cubby?"

"I have not."

"Maybe that's why you're cranky."

I had a sudden inspiration. "There was an admirable buffet in the ballroom which I had nothing to do with. Surely that wouldn't count as eating the bread of your abductors."

He looked torn, but there must have been a ravening animal in his vitals by now. "Well... I might have a small bite... only to fuel my struggle against oppression."

"That's the spirit. Let's load up a plate for you and head back to my room."

Judy smiled at me. "Yes, come dear."

And with that she wrapped her hand around my wrist like an iron shackle and calmly led me away.

We tumbled into my hotel room with a sense of relief. Bentley raised an eyebrow upon seeing Judy and myself hand in hand. Cubby retired to a corner and shoveled in the grub like it was his profession.

Suddenly the door was flung open and my aunt strode in. Her hair had escaped its carefully arranged coiffure and her gown was torn, but her glare was undiminished. She had wrapped a tablecloth around herself and resembled a Roman senator who had plans to poke some holes in Caesar after lunch. Binky slunk in behind her. Cheeseworth was practically dancing. He had a beauty of a shiner.

"What a donnybrook! One hasn't had so much fun in years! If I hadn't bwoken a nail I'd still be punching people in their widiculous faces! My word!"

"You're quite a pugilist, Cheeseworth," I said admiringly.

"Lightweight champion of my house three years wunning. When you pwesent yourself to the world as I do, you learn to defend yourself at an early age."

My aunt was attempting to recapture her stray hairs. "I knew coming to the frontier was ill-advised. Let us leave this awful place at once."

"I quite agree. Are you all right, Binky? That fellow gave you quite a kicking."

"Goodness yes. I was paddled so often as a child that I lost all feeling in my bottom by puberty. It's why I fall off of chairs so often."

"Bentley, do you want to go down to the lobby and shout for a bell person?"

"No need, Sir. I can carry the luggage myself."

"In that case, let's be off!"

At that moment Uncle Hugo, attired in his customary girdle and jodhpurs, stalked from the other room with his face red as a beet. In the hand waving over his head, I spied the Social Media King's contract.

"One moment, Sir!"

"Now Uncle..."

"Would you care to explain this? It looks very like a contract between the Social Media King and Smythe Corporation. What is the meaning of this?"

I looked around at everyone proudly. "Well... I meant it to be a surprise, but as a matter of fact I've pulled off a brilliant little piece of business. Did it all myself. No help from anyone. No need to thank me. You can congratulate me properly once we're safely airborne."

My aunt's hand darted to the emerald necklace around her neck. "We're ruined! Hugo, I refuse to sell my jewelry."

Cheeseworth stared at me gloomily. "Everything I possess is invested in Smythe Corporation stock! Without wealth I shall become ridiculous instead of amusingly eccentric."

They didn't seem to be appreciating my brilliant coup. "No, no! It's an incredible opportunity. You'll see."

Uncle Hugo raised a shaking finger. "I cannot in good conscience take another step without saying something to you, Sir."

There was a loud knocking at the door. "A moment, Uncle."

Bentley opened the door to reveal the bell person/former professor of cursive writing. He looked behind himself nervously.

"Listen, you all have to beat it! Someone in your party claimed there are nine planets and there's a mob of Eighters headed up here with tar and feathers to disagree with you."

"Quickly! Everyone! To the airfield!"

And that is how we left Manhattan: slinking out of a side door while a mob raced through the hotel, baying for our blood.

FIVE

Escape From New York

The Manhattan we drove through was a war zone. Gangs of citizens ran here and there chanting slogans like, "Eighters are Haters" and "Niners are Whiners." The occasional tomato landed on the windshield with a splat. It was with a huge sense of relief that we plunged into the tunnel below the Hudson.

New Jersey hadn't grown any cheerier. Our glittering dirigible hovered over its moorings.

We exited the car and headed for the boarding ramp, only to find our way blocked by the greasy customs inspector who had extorted us upon our arrival. The toothpick in his mouth was much the worse for wear.

"Welcome back. Good trip?"

"Tolerable. Now, my good man, if you and your grease stains would kindly take a step to the side we will be on our way."

He gazed off at the rubble piles that stretched into the distance. "Sure, but you got to pay the exit tax."

"Exit tax? How much is that?"

"Five hundred, just like before."

"Now look here..."

Bentley leaned in. "It is the custom, Sir."

The inspector carefully aimed and spat at an oil stain on the tarmac. The wind blew it wide of the mark. He sighed and shook his head. "Course you could pay it yourself at the courthouse. Should only take..."

"Fine! Pay the man, Bentley. Anything to get back in the air and away from this place!"

"New Jersey thanks you. Come again."

"Not likely. Not at these rates."

We piled into the cabin and dropped our things. The stevedores began to unmoor the blimp. I glared out the window at the customs inspector.

"I say, Binky, grab that paperweight, will you?"

He slid a large, ornamental paperweight off of the nearby desk. "Here you are."

I hefted it speculatively. "I'll bet you a tenner you can't knock the hat off that customs inspector."

Binky's eyes lit up. "It's a bet!"

I lowered the window and Binky took aim. He hurled the paperweight and we watched it conk the inspector just behind the ear. He went down with a satisfying thump and his hat rolled away into a ditch. Binky gave a little whoop.

"The hat's off. That's ten you owe me."

"It was worth it. Definitely."

The last rope was freed and we floated up into the blue. Safe at last! Cook began to lay out some snacks and there was a general air of unwinding. Judy seized my elbow in a grip that could crack a walnut.

"Why don't we go for those drinks when we land back home?"

"Why indeed?" I stammered.

She gazed at me possessively. "This has been quite a romantic adventure. Would you like to kiss me?"

My collar suddenly seemed to have shrunk. "Would I? Hmmm. Lot of people about."

"I don't mind."

To my consternation, her lips began to travel in my direction. I could see no way of evading them that would not lead to tears. Thankfully, my Uncle Hugo reared up on his hind legs again and Judy's lips were forced to retreat. My uncle cleared his throat to gain everyone's attention. "Sorry, but I was interrupted at the hotel and there are some things that must be said."

My aunt crossed her arms and glared at him. "Very well, say what you have to say and get it over with. You're like a revolutionary junta—always making declarations."

Uncle Hugo frowned. "As you know, my nephew has tried, on several occasions, to make decisions of a business nature without my advice. In every instance this has led to disaster..." I braced myself for what was coming. "...Until today! I have now perused the contract and I am happy to announce that he has struck an arrangement with the Social Media King that will bring millions, if not billions in profits to the corporation and therefore to the family. I would like to propose a toast. To Cyril!"

Aunt Hypatia beamed at me. "My jewels are safe! Well done, Nephew."

"Bwavo, Cywil!"

And with that, everyone raised a glass... to me! All except Judy. She was frowning and biting her lower lip. Finally, there was a lull in the general celebration and she cornered me by the water dispenser.

"You're going into business with that man?"

"I am."

"But he's a monster! Do you know what he does?"

"I do."

"He creates division and hate. He preys on people's insecurities."

I felt I had to speak up for my new partner. "As I understand it, he's bringing excitement into their humdrum lives."

"And you're willing to be a party to it?"

"Absolutely."

She looked at me sadly and shook her head. "I am deeply disappointed."

My ears perked up. "Are you?"

"I am. I must ask you to change your mind."

"But you heard Uncle Hugo—it's a damned fine arrangement."

"If you insist on entering into a partnership with that vile person, I can have nothing more to do with you."

"Really?"

"It is a matter of principle."

I struggled to keep a look of sad resignation on the old physiognomy. "Well, of course I'm dreadfully disappointed, but if that's how you feel then I shall respect your wishes."

She raised her chin bravely. "Thank you."

Judy moped over to an armchair and collapsed into it. Binky was on her at once like hot fudge on a sundae, leaping into the seat next to her with a look of deep empathy on his face and handing her a drink.

Cook was sidling toward me holding a tray of vegetable kabobs. "There's something I should tell you. Care for a kabob?"

"Absolutely. What is it, Cook?"

"It's onion, tomato and fennel."

"No, I mean what did you want to tell me?"

"That social media fellow tried to hire me away from you. Offered me a king's ransom."

This was appalling. I mean, I'd just stood up for the chap and here he was trying to shank me in the pancreas. "Did he? The pirate! He made off with Euphonia and now he's made an attempt on you. Got a taste for plunder, apparently."

"I thought you ought to know."

"But why didn't you go with him? You would have been rich."

"And become a slave of the oligarchs? I don't give a fig about money. I want to cook for people I care about."

A mist suddenly obscured the kabob gripped tightly in my mitt. I wiped the corner of my eye and took a nibble of fennel. Delicious! "Thank you, Cook. I'm extraordinarily moved. I hope I never give you reason to regret your faith in me."

She gave my arm a pat. "You won't. You've a good heart, dear."

"I'm dreadfully sorry if I've caused Judy any unhappiness."

"You and she were never right for each other. I've just been waiting for one of you to realize it. She'll be fine."

Cook trundled off to refill the platters. I noticed Cubby standing alone by a window, lost in thought.

"All right there, Cubby? I'm sure Euphonia is going to be happy in her new life."

"That's none of your business."

"I say, I was hoping there might be a thaw in our relationship after all we've been through."

He whirled to face me. "What have you been through? You're returning richer than you left. Some people have all the luck."

"Money isn't everything, you know."

"Don't condescend to me, Chippington-Smythe!"

"Not at all."

He drew himself up. "Nothing has changed between us. When you see me at the club, I'll thank you not to take liberties or behave as if we have any kind of understanding. The gulf between us has widened, if anything."

I sighed. "If that's the way you want it."

"It is."

"Very well. I shall treat you as the Marshall of Twits and nothing more. We shall be as strangers."

"Good!"

"Fine!"

He stalked away and snatched a large glass of water from the bar. Glaring at the platter of kabobs, he threw himself into a chair in the far corner of the cabin and hid his face behind a copy of Animatronic Horse and Hound.

Binky was weaving his way toward me with a sappy grin on his face. "She's letting me take her for drinks! Says anything's better than being alone just now."

"Sounds like you've reignited the embers of her passion, what? Well, happy endings all around. The beginnings of this odyssey were ill-omened, but it seems we have fought through with colors flying."

Binky grinned and adjusted the tie with the palm tree on it that hung around his neck. I would miss that tie.

"I'm going to the club when we land. Why not come with me?"

I shook my head solemnly. "Absolutely not! I am headed straight for bed and I'm not getting out of my pajamas until we run out of brandy."

Safe once more in my cozy little bedroom, I lolled about among the pillows and sipped a soothing cup of the old lapsang souchong. Bentley walked about picking up the various articles of clothing I had dropped.

"What joy. Why did I ever leave?"

"Indeed, Sir. It is pleasant to be home."

"Those Americans are a passionate people. Do you think they like fighting all the time?"

He stopped to consider. "Anger and resentment are commonly considered to be negative emotions."

"Why do they do it, then, do you suppose?"

"There are always those who will arouse the primitive instincts buried within the human race to amass power and wealth for themselves."

"I'm surprised they haven't attempted something of the sort here."

"Oh, they have, Sir."

I sat up and looked at him. "I don't recall ever being aware of it."

"No, Sir. I have rebuffed them."

"They've come to the door?"

"Yes, Sir. I sent them on their way and burned their periodicals as any competent valet would."

I leaned back and watched him thoughtfully. "Do you and the other servants communicate with one another, Bentley?"

"There is an informal network. We are all in agreement that we would be doing our employers a disservice if we allowed their baser emotions to be stirred in such a manner."

"Do you think I have those base emotions buried within me?"

He faced me and gave a little bow of the head. "No, Sir. You have a singular constitution."

"Thank you, Bentley. I say, that was rather lucky."

"What was, Sir?"

"That deal with the Social Media King putting the kibosh on my affair with Judy."

"Yes, I thought it might, Sir."

I sat up again and looked at him in astonishment. "Did you? Do you mean to say you planned it from the beginning?"

"We were seeking an egregious act that would induce her to reject you and this seemed to fit the bill."

"You said it was a lucrative venture."

"And so it is, Sir, but not really suitable."

"No?"

"No Sir. I'm afraid his sort of business is not the thing. It rouses the very passions you find so disturbing."

I frowned. "But how do I get out of it now?"

"Have you signed anything, Sir?"

"No, but I led him to believe that we were in business."

Bentley stood in absolute stillness for a moment. I listened to his gears grinding. Finally, he took a step toward the bed and gave a little cough.

"I should mention that the Social Media King queried me as to what emoluments would induce me to leave your employment and go to work for him."

I struggled to keep the panic out of my voice. "What?"

"I replied, of course, that no amount of money would suffice."

"Did you?"

"I did, Sir."

I stared at him, then struggled to my feet and rose to my full height in the center of the bed. "Bentley! Take a letter. To the right honorable Social Media King. Go soak your head! Sign it Cyril Chippington-Smythe and get it off in the next post."

"Thank you, Sir. I sent such a letter, couched in more diplomatic terms, before I brought your tea. Would you care for another cup?"

The End

If you enjoyed this book, please
take a moment to visit

Amazon or going to
https://www.amazon.com/dp/B0B1QWQKNL
and provide a short
review; every reader's voice is
extremely important for the life
of a book or series.

If you'd like advance notice on the next book's release
head to:

WWW.TwitsChronicles.com
where you can sign up for my email list and where you
can ask Cyril and his friends a question which they may
choose to answer in a newsletter.
I hate spam as much as you do, so I will keep emails to
a minimum.

Afterword

Cyril, Bentley and The Usual Suspects will return in:

TWITS ON THE LOOSE

The next installment of the TWITS CHRONICLES.
Read on for a taste.

Great wealth is like an ill-tempered dog. One hopes for a frolicsome companion and finds instead the teeth of responsibility locked onto one's ankle. I had recently come of age and the weight of my family's fortune had transformed me from a witty and attractive boulevardier to a hollow shell who slumped over his brandy beweeping his outcast state. Playing cards even for astronomical sums brought no flush to my cheeks. What is money when there is an endless supply of it? Friends who had always slapped one on the back and shared a scandalous tale now grew silent at my approach or tried awkwardly to touch me for a tenner to pay the bar tab. Slowly all my acquaintance drifted away. All but my cousin, Cheswick Wickford-Davies (Binky to his friends). Years of sponging had left him with no sense of shame. Hence, he was immune to the corrupting influence of wealth.

It was a gloomy morning in April when my mechanical valet, Bentley, wafted into the parlor bearing a medicinal dose of something distilled by monks in the Pyrenees and the news that Binky was champing at the bit to see me.

"Show him in, Bentley. Mr. Wickford-Davies has the run of the keep at all times."

"Very good, Sir."

Bentley floated off in that way he has and returned with Binky moping behind him.

"Hallo, old sausage! Live free or die," chirped I, cheerily.

He looked at me blankly. "What?"

"That's the new thing. 'Live free or die.' I had it from Bentley this morning."

"Not 'Confusion to our enemies'?"

I flapped a flipper breezily. "No. That's old news."

He fell heavily into a chair and rubbed his face with his hands. "Why do these mottoes always feature death so prominently?"

"I suppose because thoughts of mortality cause one to reflect. These are national slogans, you know—not advertisements for soap flakes."

He looked up at me dryly. "May I point out that the ad for Sudso soap flakes mentions plague, pestilence and flesh-eating organisms in its jingle. I think rhyming 'hysteria' with 'bacteria' is awfully good." He subsided back into melancholia.

"Was there a reason you invaded the family domicile this morning?"

He ran his fingers through his hair and groaned. "I've come to the end, Cyril. Life is a hollow shell."

I had heard this sort of thing from him too many times to be very alarmed. "Bentley? Suggestions?"

Bentley gave a judicious little nod. "Perhaps an ounce of tequila and a serotonin reuptake inhibitor?"

"Good! On the double, before he sinks into an existential fugue. These things are contagious, you know."

"At once, Sir."

Bentley disapparated like a soap bubble and I examined the patient. "Out with it, old shoe. What's got you howling at the moon?"

He gave out with another shivering groan and stared at the ceiling. "There's this girl, you see..."

Well, that was all I needed to hear. This was more or less a weekly occurrence and my patience was threadbare. "Honestly, you'd fall in love with a shovel if there was nothing else handy."

He stared at me with bloodshot eyes. "She looks right through me."

"Myopic, is she? You're rather hard to miss. Beefy, what?"

This seemed to wound him. "I've never been so thin."

"Oh, absolutely. Nearly transparent."

"I'm too miserable to eat."

Bentley shimmered into view, holding a glass of tequila and a pill on a tray. Binky took them both and downed the pill gratefully.

"Will there be anything else, Sir?"

"Nothing, Bentley, thank you."

And he was gone, just like that. Bentley could have had a brilliant career as a magician, but of course fame means nothing to a steam-powered domestic.

"Drink your tequila like a good lad. Why does your lady love treat you so spuriously?"

He slumped and sipped his drink. "It's my own fault. I have no character to speak of and she's so... good. She's given away her entire fortune to assist the downtrodden... positively destitute now."

"She sounds gruesome, if you don't mind my saying so."

"You haven't met her. One is quite helpless before the torrent of her animal spirits. She attracts more followers every day."

"Really? Who's after her—detectives, creditors?"

"Spiritual followers. People who look to her for guidance."

"She doesn't sound like your usual poison, if I may say. You've always been drawn to girls who enjoy a good rugby match and that sort of thing."

Before I could inquire further, Bentley entered the room and it is some indication of his mental agitation that I saw him coming quite clearly from the top of the stairs. The look on his face was as close to horror as the materials it was constructed of would allow.

"I beg your pardon, Sir. Did you order a... TV?"

"Is it here already? That's fast work."

He looked at me as I'm sure Caesar looked at Brutus. "There were two persons at the front door. I sent them away."

What ho, this was a little high-handed! Bentley is normally as servile as one would wish a mechanical valet to be, but every now and then he takes the bit in his teeth. "Sent them away? By what right?"

He gazed at me for a moment and I heard his gears grinding away. "A TV is... unsuitable, Sir."

Bentley tosses out the word "unsuitable" the way prisoners hurl their slops during a prison riot, but a chap has to stand up for himself now and then if he is not to become a supernumerary in his own home.

"That's hardly up to you, is it? If I want a bally TV I'll have a bally TV. Who is the employer here, you or I?"

"You, Sir," he admitted... rather reluctantly, I thought.

"You run that couple down and bring them up here at once. That's an order."

There was a further grinding of gears. "Yes, Sir."

Bentley's accustomed pace is a dignified glide, but when the occasion calls for it, he has legs like pistons. Indeed, his legs are pistons. He was out the front door like a shot and in a few moments, I heard him climbing the stairs followed by a rather flashily dressed lady and gentleman carrying large cases. He gestured to them and all but sneered.

"Your TV, Sir."

The gentleman hefted his case and looked around. "Good morning, Sir. Where shall we set up?"

"I hadn't really thought about it."

The lady staggered a bit under the weight of her cases. "What room do you frequent most?"

I thought for a moment. "The bedroom, I suppose."

She frowned. "We can't recommend the bedroom, Sir. Too stimulating."

"Oh, then I suppose... here."

This seemed to cheer them up. "Very good. Just give us a minute."

There was a flurry of activity as they disposed of their cases by the wall and did some quick stretching exercises. Adjusting their clothing, they stepped to the center of the room and cleared their throats. The gentleman began. "All right Sir, here we go. I'm Smith."

"And I'm Jones."

"And we are..."

"Thought Vacation!"

"World got you down? Portents of death and decay ruining your fun?"

"Lean back and let us take you on a Thought Vacation!"

The lady had a little clown horn with a rubber bulb which she honked a couple of times.

Binky jiggled on his toes. "Oh, I say, What fun!"

"It is fun, Sir. What would you like to see?"

I stepped forth eagerly. "What are my choices?"

"Oh, anything. We can do comedy, drama, news and weather, sports, game shows—you name it."

Binky gave a little titter. "Where on earth did you find them?"

"Cheeseworth put me on to them. TV is the latest thing. What shall we watch?"

He thought for moment. "Comedy?"

"All right." I turned to the pair. "Comedy, then."

The gentleman stepped to a case and began to snap it open. "Very good. Let me just get out our custard pies and inflated pig's bladder."

"No, it's too much bother. What about some drama?"

Now the lady ran to another case. "Of course, Sir. Where did I put that pistol? Do you mind loud noises, Sir?"

This was more complicated than I had imagined. "What can you do without props?"

The gentleman thought for a moment. "Sports? We can do bare-fisted boxing, wrestling and the long jump and for an extra fee we can acquire a ping-pong table."

The lady clasped her hands together and looked at me imploringly. "Please, Sir, not boxing. My bruises haven't healed from our last engagement."

Smith turned and growled at her. "Don't whine. I've told you to protect the body."

I thought I'd better step in. "Just the news. That doesn't require props, does it?"

"No, Sir. News it is."

The gentleman stood center and cleared his throat. He stared off into the middle distance. "The standoff continues at the Vatican. The Pope still declares that she will not wear the traditional robes and mitre because, as she puts it, 'I wouldn't wear that outfit to a hootenanny.' The College of Cardinals is taking the position that if they can wear the robe and mitre in the heat of a Roman Summer then the Pope can do so as well and if she doesn't like it she can lump it. When reminded that the Pope is infallible, they replied that infallibility only applies to dogma and not fashion."

I turned to Binky. "What do you think, old boy?"

"In local news..."

I waved at the gentleman, who was plowing ahead. "I say, you can stop for a moment."

He looked at me with disappointment. "You should say, 'Off,' Sir."

"I see. There's a protocol."

"Yes, Sir. Off, on, faster, louder, funnier... that sort of thing."

"Very well... off."

The pair backed up and stood next to their cases. The lady raised her hand. "Before we sign off may we just say that Bunbury's Lotion gives your skin that melasma-free glow that the ladies adore."

The two entertainers lost all animation and stood on the carpet rather self-consciously. Smith gave a little cough. Binky looked at me nervously.

"Well now they're just staring at us."

I addressed the pair. "Do you mean that when you're 'Off' you just stand there all day doing nothing?"

Smith shrugged. "Ours is not an easy life."

"Can't you go for a walk?"

He looked sad. "Show business, Sir."

TWITS was originally produced and distributed by Dori Berinstein, Alan Seales and the Broadway Podcast Network - the premier digital storytelling destination for everyone, everywhere who loves theatre and the performing arts. BPN.fm/Twits.

About The Author

Born in Canton Ohio and raised in a box made out of ticky-tacky, Tom Alan Robbins spent his youth as a middle-aged character actor. He has appeared in eight Broadway shows, including *The Lion King* in which he created the role of Pumbaa. He recently received a Grammy nomination for the cast album of *Little Shop of Horrors*. He has maintained a parallel career as a writer, penning scripts for TV shows like *Coach* and writing plays, one of which (*Muse*) recently won the New Works of Merit Playwriting Competition.

The Twits Chronicles series is his first attempt at novel writing and it has been a pure joy. He hopes to keep creating adventures for Cyril and Bentley as long as there are readers who enjoy them.

Also By Tom Alan Robbins

Made in the USA
Middletown, DE
13 October 2023